MW01717006

BECOMING KAREN CARTER

BOOK 2 OF THE KAREN CARTER SERIES

R.E. SARGENT

SINISTER SMILE PRESS

BECOMING KAREN CARTER

Published by Sinister Smile Press, LLC
P.O. Box 637
Newberg, OR 97132

This is a work of fiction. Names, characters, businesses, places, events, and incidents are either the products of the author's imagination or used in a fictitious manner. Any resemblance to actual persons, living or dead, or actual events is purely coincidental.

Printed in the United States of America

Trade Paperback ISBN – 978-1-953112-60-6

www.sinistersmilepress.com

contents

For Sandi–

None of this would be possible without you. You're my ride-or-die and I love you!

chapter one

Jessica Nichols sat on her back patio in her California home. She lived in the City of Orange, located in Orange County, aptly named after the citrus trees that were abundant throughout the area. As she sipped her tall glass of iced tea, she admired her dream yard. The lush green lawn that covered the almost half-acre was meticulously groomed, thanks to the hard work of her gardener, Sal. She had recently had the old lawn torn up and new sod laid down. The flowerbeds around the house were filled with zinnias, marigolds, pansies, begonias and daffodils. The array of colors, as well as the soothing sounds of the waterfall feature she recently had installed, should have carried her into a Zen-like existence, but instead, she was brooding. The day had not been kind to her.

Jessica recently finished her shift at one of the retail stores located in The Outlets at Orange, an open-air shopping center. Although she liked the company she worked for, she wasn't excited about selling apparel for the rest of her life, even though she knew she probably would not be there much longer anyway. Her manager Jordan was pretty chill and treated her well, but one of her co-workers, Stacie, drove her up the wall. Today had been worse than normal and Stacie had crossed a line. After Stacie had embarrassed her in front of a customer—to make herself look better—Jessica wanted to take her in the back room, stick her head in a mop bucket until she stopped moving and throw her in the dumpster out back. She knew that if she did not find another job soon, she would probably get herself fired. It wouldn't be the first time. Jessica had been through plenty of jobs in her short life of thirty-two years. It wasn't necessarily that she had a problem playing well with others. It was her lack of tolerance for bullshit that got her into trouble often.

Jessica took another sip of the sweet tea and returned her attention to the yard. It was the only oasis she had away from the harshness of life. While she did enjoy going to the ocean when she could, it was this little slice of heaven that kept her sane.

She had purchased the house a few years prior and felt fortunate that she could afford California real estate, especially with the limited amount of money she made. If it hadn't been for the settlement she had received when she was twenty-seven, she would most likely be in a small apartment with a roommate. With the house paid off, she only had to worry about taxes, utilities and living expenses.

With multiple glasses of tea taking effect, Jessica went inside to use the bathroom. As she came back out and walked by the doorway of the room that was across the hall, she stared at her laptop. Pausing, she felt conflicted. The evening outside was warm and inviting. Her office was darker and didn't have large amounts of sunshine streaming through the windows, mostly due to the sun being on the other side of the house. Finally, she unplugged the laptop from the power cord and the monitor cable and carried it with her. It would be a great day to work outside.

Outside, Jessica set up her laptop on the patio table and placed her tea glass next to her. The patio covering kept any sun rays from washing out her screen.

Hoping that her day would get better, she brought up her email to check for good news. Her inbox was mostly filled with junk and there was no mail to make her day brighter. A loud sigh escaped her without her even realizing it. It was the same thing every day.

Although Jessica had many things going for her—a free and clear house, good looks, and a head full of smarts—she dreamed for more. She was tired of working dead-end jobs to pay the bills. She knew she had real talent, but no one seemed to want to give her a shot.

Jessica brought up a spreadsheet that she was using to track query letters sent to literary agents. She had written three novel-length manuscripts, hoping to get them published. It wasn't just her dream—she felt an ache inside that was indescribable. She wanted it more than anything else she had ever wanted before. She had to have it. She just could not seem to catch a break.

In the past few years, she had read dozens of books and online articles about getting published. Most sources suggested finding a literary agent first, who would then help find a publisher to buy the rights. Two huge barriers to overcome, yet she could not even get past the first one. Every week, she sent out five queries—some by email and others the old-fashioned way. According to her spreadsheet, she had sent out over three hundred and forty queries over the years, but unfortunately, she only had a seventeen percent response rate. How was she ever supposed to make her dream happen if she didn't know what she was doing wrong?

The more she researched, the more frustrated she became. She had re-written her query letter a dozen times trying to make it as eye-catching as possible. She changed up the design to give the emails a level of professionalism. For the printed versions, she used expensive paper as well. She had no idea how she would catch someone's attention if they wouldn't read her work.

Out of the responses she did get, most of the emails were a canned reply thanking her for her submission and simultaneously letting her know they had no interest in her projects. The mailed responses were even fewer and typically came back with a form letter, although one agent had simply written 'Sorry, not for us!' in red letters across the face of her own query letter, before mailing it back.

Twice, an agent had requested more information. One wanted the first three chapters and the other had asked for the full manuscript. Neither one had decided to sign her though.

Worried that the quality of her work was lacking, she asked anyone that was interested to read one or all of her manuscripts. Along the way, she received feedback that she took to heart and incorporated into her writing, but the general consensus was that her work was strong, getting better with each one she wrote.

Jessica had started her fourth novel a few weeks prior, but she lost motivation recently. Her confidence was lacking and she wondered if she was simply wasting her time. Maybe her work was shit after all and people were just being nice. Why write a fourth when she couldn't get anyone to look at the first three?

Defeated, Jessica closed her laptop, took it back inside and sat it on the kitchen island. She felt like giving up, yet she was terrified that there was nothing more to life than working a dead-end job and paying bills. There had to be something else, yet she couldn't seem to gain entry to the club she so desperately wanted to belong to.

Spotting the current book she was reading, she picked it up and went back out on the patio. She needed an escape and reading never failed her.

chapter **two**

As she squinted to read the words of the book, Jessica realized the sun had slipped below the horizon and it was dusk. She had lost track of all time and had not noticed it was getting late around her. Gathering her empty glass, she went back inside and fixed herself something to eat and got ready for bed. She had to be at work to open the store the next day.

In bed, she resumed her reading, enthralled with the mystery that she was trying to solve in her mind. She had recently discovered this particular author, Karen Carter, and had a hard time putting down her books each time she started one. She had read seven of them so far and she knew there were more that she hadn't read yet.

Reading had shaped her childhood. She remembered her daddy reading to her every night at bedtime, without fail. When she had learned to read on her own, she would sneak a flashlight into her room and read under the covers when she was supposed to be sleeping. She had loved books ever since. In high school—during her awkward phase, before she blossomed into a beautiful young woman—books were her escape from the constant teasing she received over her boyish figure, acne and braces. If the haters could see her now.

As she read deeper into the story, she was in awe over the writing, and she appreciated it. Authors like this had greatly influenced her own writing. In fact, her deep ache to become an author stemmed from reading her favorite authors. Karen Carter was fast becoming her idol though and she would read everything she could find by her.

At thirteen minutes after one, her eyes popped open and she realized that she had dozed off in the middle of a page. Sliding her bookmark in between the pages to hold her spot, she slid the paperback onto her nightstand and clicked off the light. She would have to solve the mystery the next night.

The next morning after getting ready for work, she examined herself in the mirror. She tucked her long blonde hair back behind her ear and made sure her clothes were not inside out or something similarly embarrassing. Satisfied with the way the clothes complimented her thin frame, she left for work, which was only a ten-minute drive.

At work, she found a parking spot easily as the shops had not opened yet and the barrage of customers would arrive later. She opened the store, locked the door and deactivated the alarm system before it triggered a response to the call center.

Opening duties were fairly easy for this job. She wasn't considered a manager, but she was a key holder. She simply had to log on to the registers, put the tills inside the cash drawers and make sure that everything had been put back in its place the night before. At opening time, she would turn on all the lights, the in-store music and unlock the doors.

She was expecting another employee to come in around opening time, but her face fell when Stacie walked through the door.

"What are you doing here?" Jessica snapped. She didn't even think about trying to hide her bitchiness.

"I work here; what do you think?" Stacie snapped back.

"I thought Kevin was working this morning."

"We switched. Now you have to put up with my ass."

Stacie walked towards the back room to drop off her purse.

"The building isn't big enough to contain that huge ass," Jessica muttered under her breath.

Stacie stopped and walked back towards Jessica.

"What did you say, Bitch?"

"I said no one should have to put up with an ass that size. Your poor husband."

"I'm gonna mess you up," Stacie promised, charging towards Jessica with arms outstretched.

"What's going on here?" Jordan called out, panic edging into his voice.

Not realizing he had even come in, both girls immediately paused and swiveled towards the door. Silence greeted Jordan.

"Maybe you guys didn't hear me. What's happening?"

"This bitch is out of line," Stacie offered.

"See what I have to put up with?" Jessica combatted. She put on her best innocent face. "She threatened to kick my ass after I simply said good morning to her."

"Friggin liar," Stacie snarled, hatred flooding from her eyes.

"Go home, Stacie. You're out of control," Jordan demanded.

"Me? I'm out of control? Everything was fine when I came to work and she provoked me! She needs to go, not me."

Jessica smiled sweetly. "I provoked you by saying good morning?"

Unable to contain herself any longer, Stacie ran at Jessica and knocked her on her ass, her hands around her throat.

"Stupid Bitch! I hate you. I wish Jordan had never hired you."

As she lay on the ground looking up at Stacie, who was sitting on top of her, she smiled, even though the force of her landing on her back had racked her spine with a trail of pain, and the hands around her throat were causing her extreme discomfort. It was mere seconds before Jordan reached them and pulled Stacie off of her. It took another five minutes to calm her down and get Jessica off the floor.

Locking the front door to keep customers from entering, Jordan made sure Stacie stayed seated in the back room while he attended to Jessica.

"Do you want me to call someone to have you checked out?"

"Probably not a bad idea," she answered, grimacing from the pain that raced up her spine.

Jordan walked to the phone.

"Might want to call the police also. I'm pressing assault charges as well."

Jordan stopped, a puzzled look on his face.

"Seriously?" he asked.

"As a heart attack. You did just see her jump me, right?"

"Well yeah, but…"

"But what, Jordan? Assault is illegal."

"But she is your coworker. Do you really want to bring this kind of attention to the situation?"

"Sounds like you want to brush it under the carpet."

"Nnoo," he stammered. "I just thought . . ."

Jessica interrupted him. "Thought what? That I would be okay with being knocked to the floor and choked?"

"It's not like that."

"Then what's it like, Jordan? I'm sure the store

video will back up my allegations." Jessica nodded towards the nearest camera, a small black dome mounted to the ceiling tile.

Jordan paused, unsure of what to do.

"Let me make it easy for you. You call them, or I will."

A sigh escaping his lips, Jordan walked to the register counter and picked up the phone, dialing nine-one-one.

chapter three

Jessica popped the lid off the bottle of Norco that was on her bedside nightstand. She dropped two of them in her mouth and chased them with a drink of water. She tried to get comfortable, but the pain had set in again. Wincing, she waited while the pills took their time, blocking some of the pain sensors.

While the attack at the store had ended as quickly as it had started, it was the action of landing flat on her back and head—after being in an upright position—that had done a number on her. Jessica had been transported by ambulance to Chapman Global Medical Center. They had checked her out, taken several x-rays as well as performed a CT scan on her head. After a few hours of monitoring her, and pumping her full of fluids and painkillers, they sent her home for bed rest. It had been over twenty-four hours since the incident, yet Jessica was still in extreme amounts of pain.

Jordan had come to see her at the hospital before she was released. She was surprised to see that he was actually finally taking the situation seriously. Stacie had been arrested and Jordan had fired her. While at the hospital, he had her sign some paperwork to open a workman's compensation claim. She was off work until she felt better. He had even given her a ride home when she was released.

The melodic tone of her cell phone woke her up and she hadn't realized that she had even dozed off. Shaking off her sleep fog, she answered it.

"Hi Jessica. Brent Jenkins from Jenkins Law Firm. Do you remember me?"

"Of course. That's why I left a message on your web site."

"Very good. It's been a long time. How are you doing?"

"I've been better."

"What's going on?"

"Pardon me if I sound woozy. I'm on Norco and I just woke up."

"No worries. Norco? What happened?"

Jessica explained how Stacie had attacked her.

"Did you press charges?"

"Oh, heck, yes. She was arrested."

"Excellent. I assume you want to go after her?"

"Not just her. The company."

"Tell me your thought process here."

"They failed to keep me safe. They should have known she was dangerous. She attacked me right in front of my manager."

"It really depends on what a jury believes. If they believe her story over yours, we might be wasting our time."

"It was all captured on the store video system."

Brent let out a low whistle. "If the video shows exactly what you described to me, we have something. If we can prove they knew she was dangerous, we have so much more."

"That's my hope."

"I'll get started on submitting a subpoena to get that video, before it disappears."

"Thanks, Brent. You have always taken care of me."

"You don't have much luck when it comes to work, do you?"

Jessica paused. "It would seem not," she responded, almost whispering it.

"Sorry," Brent apologized. "I should never have

brought that up. I know that was pretty traumatizing for you."

"It's okay. It happened. It's part of who I am. I can't erase the memory even though I've tried. It's with me forever."

"I'm just glad he paid the price."

"Me too."

"Okay, let me get started on this and I will get back in touch with you. Feel better."

"I plan to, eventually."

They said their goodbyes and Jessica ended the call. Placing her phone back on the nightstand, she closed her eyes again and thought about the last time she had worked with Brent Jenkins.

Five years prior when she was in her late twenties, Jessica had worked for a startup company and was the assistant to the president. She had actually been offered the position while she was a barista at Starbucks. Every morning, she made him a venti vanilla latte and every morning, he added a five-dollar bill to the tip jar. Back then, she had only known him as 'Jerry'—the name that was written on the cup day after day. After a year of coming in, Jerry asked her if he could buy her a cup of coffee after her shift. It was then he proposed the assistant position to her. At first blush, she politely refused the offer, while thanking him profusely for his confidence in her; however, as he stubbornly added numbers to the salary he offered, she quickly changed her mind.

The first six months went well for her, even though the number of hours she was putting in was ridiculously heavy, but things started slowly changing as she noticed him first complimenting her often and then openly flirting with her. She brushed off his open affection as nothing more than an innocent annoyance, until the night it happened.

Jerry had landed a new contract with a supplier and he and Jessica were working late to finalize the deal. The rest of the office had left around eight p.m., but Jessica and Jerry kept at it until almost midnight. As exhaustion crept in, Jessica stretched out on the office couch to rest her eyes. Her mistake was falling asleep.

Jessica felt a tear slide down her cheek as she remembered how she had been woken up. She still felt dirty five years later. When she popped awake on that couch, all those years ago, her blouse was unbuttoned, her bra had been pulled up and Jerry was openly masturbating over her. Instinct taking over, Jessica had punched him hard in the junk and as he collapsed, she ran towards the elevator, hoping to get away and never come back. She panicked as the car took its sweet time to get to her floor. When the doors finally opened, her breath rushed from her lungs, relief setting in.

Rushing inside, she hammered on the buttons to close the doors and return to the lobby. As they finally slid closed, she screamed as an arm slid between the two heavy pieces of metal, causing them to pop open again. Standing on the other side was Jerry, an enraged look on his face.

The rest of her memory was a blur, but it consisted of him dragging her out of the elevator and back to his office. It took two hours for him to torture her with every perversion he wanted to act out, and when he was done, she was used, battered and torn. When he was finished, he simply got up, got dressed and left the building, all without saying a word.

Shuddering from the brutality of the memory, Jessica tried to convince herself that the end result made up for the transgression. Jerry had been arrested and ended up in prison. The lawsuit that she had hit him with bankrupted the business, but she had come out three-quarters of a million dollars richer from the ordeal. She was happy it had paid for the house, but sometimes the house triggered the memory of the brutal rape.

It wasn't until after that incident that Jessica's

views had changed. The biggest loss for her was that she could not trust anyone. For that reason, she shied away from people and had a hard time building relationships at work. It wasn't until after the rape that she had a hard time keeping any one job. She was screwed up and she knew it. Her only escape was books. Whether she was reading them or writing them, they were her life. She didn't need the rest of the world and all of the attached bullshit. She simply needed words to hold her and make her feel right.

Jessica's headache returned and she was brought back to the current situation. There was no way she would be going back to that job. Not after she soaked them for as much as she could. Her thoughts turned to Stacie. She had never liked that bitch and was pretty pleased at the way the situation had played out. Now she had a record and was unemployed. Even with her headache attacking her, a smile spread across her face as she once again fantasized about ways she could off Stacie. If only murder was legal.

chapter four

After a few days, Jessica started to feel good enough to get out of bed, even though she still had aches and pains. She had finished the Karen Carter book and had started the next one. The more she read, the more she realized they both had a similar voice in their writing styles. She wondered why Karen Carter was so successful and she could not even get anyone to look seriously at her work. It just wasn't fair. Then it hit her. Why not submit a query to Karen Carter's agent? She would be sure to love her work if she loved Karen's.

Remembering that Karen had dedicated one of her books to her literary agent, Jessica grabbed all of her Carter books and started paging through them until she found the one she wanted. With the agent's name at hand, she Googled it and found the literary agency she represented. The agency website had contact information for each agent. Jessica pasted one of her favorite query letters into the body of the email and customized it to make it more personable. After she had read it multiple times, she clicked send. She had nothing to lose. The worst that could happen would be to hear the word 'no' again.

Excused from work for a while, with no true intention of actually going back, Jessica decided to resume work on her fourth book. She could not let her treatment by literary agents affect her writing habits. With each book she wrote, she finely honed her skills. When she finally did get picked up, she would be able to publish often since she had a backlog of manuscripts.

Jessica typed a paragraph and reread it. Unsatisfied with the flow of the prose, she worked at it to smooth it out, but she was having a hard time concentrating. Her thoughts turned back to Karen Carter. She appeared to be about the same age from the author photo, but the main difference was Karen was successful and living her dream and Jessica was simply living her life off of the proceeds from lawsuits filed against people that made stupid decisions. Even if she made bank off of this recent incident, the money would eventually dry up and she would be back working some mindless job. She absolutely had to figure out how to become a best-selling author.

Lost in the fantasy of what it would be like to make it, Jessica pulled up the Karen Carter website and looked through each page. While most of the material was related to her books, there was some information about the author. If the bio was correct, she lived in Manhattan. Intrigued, she performed an online search for 'Karen Carter Author' to see what other online information she could find.

Pages of related links came up from her search. Methodically, she clicked on each one, looking at the content. Book sales pages, reviews, blogs and tons of other content came up, none of it useful in learning more about her favorite author. Finally, on the tenth page, she came across a news article talking about how the author had been picked up by Random House years earlier when she had submitted her first series. The article went into how long the much-younger author had been writing and trying to become published, before she was actually picked up. Their stories were similar. If Karen Carter could do it, so could she.

Unable to find any other useful information on

the author, Jessica went back to the Carter website and looked back through all of the information. Nothing else caught her attention until she noticed the contact page. It was then that it hit her. She would try to establish contact with the author and see if she could worm her way into the industry that way. She clicked on the form, entered her contact information and a message, praising Karen for her outstanding body of work. When she was satisfied with her message, she clicked send.

As she closed her web browser, she wondered if she would get a response. It seemed like nothing quite worked out for her, but she knew if she stopped trying, she would certainly never have a chance.

With concentration eluding her, she went back to reading instead of writing. She read for a couple of hours before her phone pulled her out of the world she was entrenched in.

"Hello?"

"Jessica, Brent Jenkins."

"Hey."

"Good news."

"What's up?"

"We got the subpoena for the video."

"No shit?"

"No shit. It will be served to your employer tomorrow. We will be filing suit next week as well, as long as that's still what you want to do."

"Yes, that's exactly what I want. Do you need anything from me?"

"I'll send over the papers before we file them, for you to check accuracy. Other than that, once we know the court date, we'll need to prepare for trial."

"What's the number?"

"It won't be anywhere as much as last time."

"I figured."

"I was going to try for five-hundred grand and hope we get half of that."

"I'm good with that. Just remember that the more I get, the more you get."

"Trust me, that's never something I would forget."

"Again, I figured."

"Talk to you soon, Jessica. By the way, you feeling any better?"

"A little. I'm out of bed anyway. The bruises on my neck are pretty intense though. I'm glad we have plenty of pictures."

"Me too. The worse it looks, the better off we will be. Get some rest."

"Thanks, Brent. See ya."

"Bye."

Jessica ended the call and smiled. If she could get another chunk of money, hopefully she wouldn't have to work for a while, which would give her more time to work on getting published. She needed all of the time—and all of the luck—she could conjure up.

chapter five

When the lawsuit was filed the following week, one of the claims was that Jessica suffered from post-traumatic stress disorder over the incident, causing her to suffer anxiety over going back to work. To back up her claims, she started seeing a therapist, to whom she recounted the horrific story of her attack at work. Between the workman's compensation claim and the lawsuit, the company didn't dare chance terminating her employment and she continued to get paid.

With plenty of spare time on her hands, Jessica continued to work on her fourth novel, when she wasn't reading one of the Karen Carter books she devoured as quickly as possible. She knew that if she didn't slow down, she would run out of new books to read, which would be problematic. She didn't necessarily want to start reading a new author. It was way too much of a commitment.

Two weeks after the incident at work, she opened her email to find four different messages that caught her attention. The first two were responses from literary agents that she had queried sometime in the past month. Both of them were boilerplate rejection letters. The third one was from Karen Carter's agent. Nervous, she paused, afraid to open it. Inhaling deeply, she double-clicked the message. As she read it, her hopes once again fell, although this one wasn't exactly a rejection. The email stated that she was not accepting any new clients at this time. One more door closed in her face. Although she knew she should be upset, she felt her heart pounding and it was then she realized that she was extremely anxious over the last email; one from Karen Carter. She paused and then finally opened it. She certainly didn't think she would get a response and especially not a personalized one, but it appeared that was the case. As she read the email, she was in awe.

Dear Jessica,

Thanks for your kind email. It's fans like you that give me the motivation to do what I do every day. I'm glad you are enjoying the latest series. It's my favorite one so far. You never know what could happen next. For that matter, sometimes even I don't know what will happen next. Maybe we'll find out together!

All my best,

Karen Carter

Jessica was floored by the email. She had never talked to a real celebrity before. Okay, so she hadn't actually talked to her, but an email was a close second. While the rest of the emails weren't encouraging, her spirits were lifted to know that her favorite author, no matter how busy she was, had reached out to her. Intending to frame the letter at some point in time, Jessica hit the print button, spooling the email to the printer.

Motivated again, Jessica returned to her latest novel. It was time to get serious about it. She again hoped she could befriend Karen and use her as an in to a publishing contract. She seemed to be running out of other options.

Strategic about her plan, Jessica waited two weeks before she emailed Karen Carter back. She had finished one of Karen's books during that time and used the situation as an excuse to reach out and give feedback on how much she had enjoyed it. Attached to the email, she added an animated GIF of a cartoon character hugging a book. She hoped that Karen would get a kick out of it.

Three weeks later, she was shocked to find another email from Karen Carter in her inbox. She had given up on getting a response, not that she had expected one. As an author that put out three books a year, Karen had to be extremely busy. The sight of the email sitting there waiting to be opened filled her with joy. She clicked.

Dear Jessica,

Thanks for your last email. Once again, you are very kind with your compliments. I'm so glad you enjoyed yet another of my books. I have to admit the animation you sent was cute, cute, cute! Thanks for the smile.

All my best,

Karen Carter

Jessica giggled when she read the message. It was happening. She was building a friendship. She would build a connection with Karen Carter if it killed her.

That night, Jessica woke up from a dead sleep, her heart beating rapidly. She didn't understand what had awakened her. She sat in the dark and listened for something, anything. She heard nothing.

Straining to make sense of things, her dream came back to her, overwhelming her. It had been so real. In her dream, she and Karen Carter were hanging out, going out to dinner together, hitting clubs in New York City, catching movies together and palling around like they had known each other all of their lives. In one part of her dream, Karen had confided her deepest, darkest secret, but for the life of her, Jessica could not remember what the secret was.

Trying to recall the rest of the dream, Jessica got up and made her way to the kitchen, pulling a pint of Ben and Jerry's strawberry cheesecake out of the freezer. She absent-mindedly ate from the container, picking her way through the dream, hoping to remember what the big secret was. If the secret had truly been revealed to her in her dream, her subconscious certainly had a tight lock on the information. She wasn't able to recall what was said.

Full, she snapped the lid back on the ice cream and put the pint back in the freezer. Returning to bed, she tried to go back to sleep, but her mind would not let loose of the unusual dream. Her thoughts toyed with the idea of her and Karen actually being friends, hanging out like it was the most natural thing in the world. She realized she was being silly by even fantasizing about it. It would never happen. Still, it had seemed real and she reveled in the thought. As she went to sleep again for the night, the dream did not return.

The next morning, Jessica woke up later than normal. She felt drained, as if she hadn't slept for a week. The event from the previous night came back to her and, instead of feeling the elation she had felt after awakening during the night, she felt a sadness. She couldn't place her finger on what was wrong as the feeling hid at the edge of her consciousness, teasing her. Many times, as she tried to snatch the thought from the back of her mind to bring it to her conscious mind, it quickly retreated further back in the depths.

As she made breakfast, she fussed over what was weighing on her, but she still couldn't put her finger on it. By the time she was cleaning up the kitchen, her bewilderment turned to frustration, but she was still stuck on what the issue was. It wasn't until much later in the afternoon, when she was standing in the shower letting the near-scalding water cascade over her body, that she realized what was bothering her.

She would never hang out with Karen Carter. They would never be friends. In Karen's emails, she was simply being nice. Once again, Jessica realized that her life would never amount to anything more than it was now. What she didn't know is how she would be able to cope with being nothing, now and forever.

chapter six

The following week was a difficult one. Jessica sunk into a depression unlike any she had ever been in before. She didn't understand why. In the past, she had been raped brutally. She had been choked out by a co-worker. Her life was not even close to what she wanted, and she had never before felt so low. This was a new one for her.

By Wednesday, Jessica was shocked to find that she smelled like stale sweat and even more so to realize she hadn't showered in days. She got out of bed, threw her pajamas and her bed sheets into the washing machine and hopped in the shower. Being smelly was not something she was okay with.

After a hot, relaxing shower, and remaking the bed with fresh sheets, Jessica looked around her house and grimaced. She had been letting it go as well. Dishes languished in the sink, unopened mail spread across the counter, and shoes sat helter-skelter by the front door—just a general messiness that wasn't her style. Her anger boiled up inside of her as she cursed herself for being sad and pathetic. She had always been a fighter, so why was she sitting there feeling sorry for herself when she should be channeling her energy into doing something that would change her life?

Motivated to break the cycle, Jessica turned on her Bluetooth speaker and set her iPhone to randomly play her library of songs by Pink, who had always been a huge inspiration to her. The grit and passion behind the lyrics were something that resonated with her and with the music blasting in the background, in four hours, she had her house back to the way she preferred it, including the last load of laundry tumbling in the dryer.

Taking a break, Jessica poured herself a glass of tea and went out to her patio. A Hooded Oriole hopped along the grass, presumably looking for a worm. She marveled over its bright orange body and black wings. It was the only other inhabitant of the back yard.

Determined to change her future, Jessica watched the bird—who she quickly named Frank—and tried to come up with a plan for her life. She started sorting through what was wrong and what was right about it. She made a mental checklist of the good things: she lived in a warm climate, had her own house which was paid off, was still fairly young and attractive and she considered herself to be extremely smart.

On the downside, she didn't like any of the jobs she worked and didn't have the patience or confidence to try for something better. Truth be told, her position of Assistant to the President of the company looked great on a resume, but even thinking about the situation gave her nausea and she surely didn't want others asking her why she quit, so she left it off of her resume. She laughed to herself as she envisioned the conversation. *Oh, I left that job, because the president of the company brutally raped me, so I put him in prison and sued, making me rich and forcing the company to go under.* Yes, that would be a great way to get hired.

If she were to be honest with herself, she didn't like working for others. Only writing made sense to her. The problem was, writing would never pay the bills if she couldn't get published and she would have to work jobs she hated. She realized then that the only real thing wrong with her life was that she wasn't published. If she could figure out that problem, everything else in her life would fall into place.

"What should I do, Frank?" she asked the bird, who was in no hurry to leave the yard.

The bird stopped what it was doing and cocked its head towards her, perhaps wondering what she was saying. As she watched, it turned its attention back to the grass, pecked a few times in succession and raised its head, a thin, wriggling worm dangling from its beak. Satisfied with its prize, the Oriole flew off.

"Bye, Frank. Thanks for the chat," Jessica said to no one in particular.

She thought about the worm that Frank had just caught to procure food for its family. Although Frank was probably a Francine instead, it knew what it wanted, poised itself to grab it when it could and, when the time was right, it snatched the worm. Jessica knew that she too needed to find her worm. She simply had to poise herself and get ready.

Jessica thought about Karen Carter and how much she enjoyed her books. She felt an admiration that was deep. She wanted to be just like Karen. Hell, she actually wanted to be her. She seemed to have everything. Maybe the key to getting everything she wanted was to find out everything she could about Karen Carter, which might get her insider information on how she could get discovered. She was confident that if she could just catch a break, she would be successful. She thought about her emails back and forth between herself and Karen. They were certainly spread out and there was no way a famous author would befriend her. She was simply being nice. There had to be a way she could find out more.

Not sure which direction to turn, Jessica went inside and logged on to her laptop. Google was her friend when she was trying to figure things out. She entered the phrase "how to find out everything about someone" and searched. The search came back with approximately eight-hundred and sixty-four million results. She would be busy for a while.

Jessica sat at the kitchen island and started scrolling through the results, clicking on the links that were intriguing. She perused pages about private investigators and websites that provided a view into people's hidden information. There were certainly different options available.

For the next couple of hours, she researched different links and bookmarked sites that she felt she might want to come back to later. Her eyes were starting to get blurry and she was just about to log off for the night when she spotted something different. A spy website. She scrolled past it and then scrolled back, her interest piqued. She clicked the link. As she read through the site, she was shocked at all the spy tools that the company sold, but the one that caught her interest the most was a computer monitoring software that not only logged keystrokes from the keyboard, but also provided a live view of the activity on the host computer, sending it to the person watching the activity. Suddenly, she wasn't tired any longer.

As she compared products, her mind raced. If she could simply see everything that Karen Carter typed and the sites she went to, she could easily learn everything about her, including her address, her personal information and her correspondence with her agent and publisher. This information could really help her in her quest to get noticed. She clicked on the product she liked the most and read through the details. Her heart fell when she read that the software would have to be installed on the computer first. There was no way she could do that. That would entail finding out Karen's address and breaking into her house. She would also have to know her password to log on. It would never happen.

Frustrated, she clicked the 'contact' button and sent a message to the company asking if there was any other way to install the software, stating that her husband and his computer were currently in another state. She gave her email and phone contact information and, discouraged, shut down her computer. She would call it a night and approach it the next morning with a clear head.

As Jessica was brushing her teeth, she heard her cell phone ringing in the bedroom. Spitting out the toothpaste in her mouth and performing a quick rinse, she ran to the phone and answered it.

"Hello?"

"Hi, is this Jessica Nichols?" He spoke quickly, but she had no problem understanding him.

"This is her. Who's calling?"

"My name is Jesse. I'm returning your call regarding your recent inquiry on our computer monitoring software. I hope it isn't too late?" His last statement was more of a question.

"I was just going to bed. You guys work this late?"

"We're actually located in Finland. I figured since you just sent a message, you were up. I hope I didn't disturb you."

"It's fine. I'm curious if there are any other options for installing the software. I can't exactly install it in person."

There was a brief pause on the line before Jesse answered.

"Yes, there's another method, but it isn't listed on our website."

"Well what is it?" Jessica asked, excitement building in her voice.

"It's a little unorthodox, even for us."

"I'm still listening."

"We can pack the program in an attachment, much like a virus. When they click on the attachment, it will install the program in the background."

"Is it discoverable?"

"Only if someone is a computer expert. Even virus protection won't see it."

"I'm not a computer expert myself, but don't you have to send an executable file in order for it to deploy?"

"Yes, but we can mask the file so that it doesn't look like one. It can simply be a picture file."

"So, I send it, they open it, they go on with their life and know nothing about it?"

"Correct."

"And how long will it work?"

"As long as they don't have a hard drive crash or restore their computer to factory settings, it should work as long as the computer is still in service."

"And I can just log in from my computer, undetected?"

"Correct again."

"How do I sign up? I'm in."

"Excellent, Ms. Nichols. There are a few things you should know. First of all, please send us a photo image that you want to use to deploy the program. I just sent you an email that you can reply to with the image. As soon as we get it, we will pack it with the program and send it back to you, most likely within twenty-four hours."

"Thanks. I'll send you something tomorrow."

"Excellent. Secondly, when you get an email back from us, there will be the picture file and a PDF document with instructions for accessing the computer you deploy the program to. Please do not click on the photo yourself, or it will deploy the software to your computer. Simply save the file to your computer and attach it to any email."

"Sounds easy. Anything else?"

"Two things. Go ahead and place your order online for the package available. When you get to checkout, enter the following promo code. S-P-E-C-I-A-L-P-2-0. This will signify that you want the special package we discussed. Secondly, make sure your save the files to your computer within forty-eight hours of receiving them. The email messages are designed to auto delete forty-eight hours after receipt."

"Got it. Thanks for the clear instruction. I will place the order tonight before bed."

"The instructions will cover the same information, but I thought it would be good to tell you as well in case you don't get to it right away."

"Thanks for your help, Jesse. You made my night."

"Glad I could help. Is there anything else I can help you with?"

"All good. Thanks. Goodnight."

Jesse chuckled. "It's day here, but goodnight to you."

Jessica laughed at her mistake. "Bye."

After ending the call, Jessica went back to her computer and to the site she had researched earlier. She easily found the monitoring software and added it to the cart. At checkout, she entered the promo code and finished the transaction, paying with her Visa card. She was looking forward to morning for the first time in a long time.

chapter seven

The next morning, Jessica rolled out of bed the first time she opened her eyes. She was excited to get started with her research. If Karen Carter could do it, so could she. She just needed to figure out how.

Upon checking her email, she found the request for the photo file that the program would be imbedded in. She knew that Karen had opened an attachment she had sent prior, so she was hoping she would open another one. She only needed it to happen one more time.

As she searched the internet, she looked at image after image of funny sayings, inspirational quotes and everything in between.

After a couple of hours, she settled on a quote that talked about the magic of an author's words.

After saving it to her computer, she sent a reply to Jesse's email and attached the photo. Now to wait the twenty-four hours. She hoped it would show up sooner as she was impatient. She knew it was night time in Finland and when Jesse got the email, it would be Friday morning. She hoped she would not have to wait until Monday to get the file.

With nothing else to do, she contacted her lawyer to talk about the lawsuit. She ended up having to leave a message for him, but when he called her back, he had promising news. There were discussions about the company making a settlement offer to keep the case out of court. She was hoping that would be the case since a trial would be a lot of work, not to mention stressful.

Feeling like things were finally going right for once, Jessica felt giddy. She decided to get out for a while since she had been cooped up in the house for a long time. Her first stop was Target where she browsed the store, adding an occasional item to her cart. When she passed the apparel department, she spotted a cute pair of black jeans that called out to her. When she tried them on, they fit her body perfectly, clinging tightly to her legs and butt as she hoped they would. In love with her new pants, she found a blouse and a pair of shoes that complemented the jeans. The outfit was a gift to herself and she was happy it was something she could wear in a casual setting or even a dressier one.

After leaving Target, Jessica stopped by the Ralph's grocery store that was closest to her house. Her refrigerator was getting bare and needed some love. When she couldn't get anything more in the cart, she decided to call it a day and head to the checkout. She marveled over the fact that grocery shopping for one person could result in such a huge purchase.

On the way home from the store, Jessica pulled through Wienerschnitzel and grabbed a few chili-cheese dogs on pretzel buns. They were one of her guilty pleasures.

Back at home after she put the groceries away and ate, she worked on her latest novel, which she was almost finished with. She hoped to have the first draft finished in two weeks, when she would then go back and finesse it.

After a few hours of writing, Jessica watched some television in the living room, channel surfing until she came across a movie that she hadn't seen in a long time. Anxious to get the file, the movie helped take her mind off of things. Even if Jesse and the team had started work already, she had no right to expect that she would be the first customer that was taken care of. Patience was not a quality she was long on.

When the movie was over, Jessica checked her email from her phone. There was nothing but junk mail in her inbox. Deciding that she could either stay up all night obsessing, or go to bed and hope to find the files in the morning, she chose the latter.

In bed for the night, she turned on the bedroom television and found a reality show for background noise. She watched for a while and slipped into slumber just as a fight broke out on the show. The bleeps that censored the language serenaded her as she fell into a deep sleep.

In the morning, she woke early from a full bladder. Typically, when that happened, she would relieve herself and head back to bed, but she was anxious to find out if the file had arrived, so she checked her phone while she peed. She let out a little shriek when she saw it. An email from Jesse with two attachments.

Almost forgetting to flush, Jessica ran out into the living room and retrieved her laptop, bringing it back into the bedroom with her. She opened the PDF and read the instructions to make sure she didn't make any mistakes. Confident she understood what actions to take, she saved both documents in a folder on her laptop named "Karen Carter."

Twice she had written Karen and twice she had received a response. She hoped that there would be a third time. Hell, she didn't even need a response. All she needed was for Karen to click on the attachment and open the picture. The program would do the rest.

As she wrote her third email, she paused, feeling slightly guilty. Karen Carter had been nothing but kind to her and she was basically sending her a virus to spy on her to better her own life. She felt a little despicable over her plan yet when she reconsidered it, she saw no other alternative to get what she wanted—what she needed. Desperate to change her life, she finished the email, attached the file and clicked send. It was now just a waiting game.

Five weeks went by with no response from Karen. Jessica checked her email multiple times a day for the first week and then tapered back to a couple times daily. She also tried following the instructions on how to access the host computer, but when she tried, no connection was made. Either Karen had not clicked on the image or the software didn't work. She would never know unless she heard back from Karen.

By week seven, Jessica had given up being contacted by Karen. Her employer had settled out of court for one hundred and seventy-three thousand dollars and she had promptly quit after taking the payout. Knowing she would most likely have to start working again after the money was gone, she decided to write full-time while she could, and continue to work on getting published. There seemed to be no other options available to her.

In September, Jessica was finished with her fourth manuscript and partially done writing her fifth. She received great joy pouring her heart into her writing yet she felt empty as the words sat unread, buried in a file inside her computer. The art she created with her mind should be read by the world, but instead, it had no purpose. Maybe she was just kidding herself after all. Maybe she didn't have what it takes.

On September fifteenth, Jessica got up late, a lack of motivation taking hold of her. Depression had started to take over once again and she knew it was simply a matter of time before she had to go back to work. By her calculations, she had another two years before the money ran dry. If she wasn't making money from her writing by then, she would probably never make it.

After a few hours of watching TV, Jessica decided to check her email. It had been a couple of days. As she deleted the junk out of her box, she saw it in the nick of time, almost deleting it in the process. It was an email from Karen Carter, months after she had sent the file attachment. Jessica stared at the email for a couple of minutes, anxious about opening it. What if she knew what Jessica had done? Finally, she clicked it open and read the message.

Dear Jessica,

I have to tell you how sorry I am that it took me so long to respond to you. I had two deadlines looming as well as a couple of things I had to handle. Thanks again for your nice email. You never fail to put a smile on my face with your cute little pictures. Until next time.

All my best,

Karen Carter

Jessica stared at the screen in disbelief. Could it be possible? Had Karen Carter actually downloaded the program into her computer? She knew there was only one way to find out, yet she was nervous. What if she could detect it on the other end? Even if she did, could it be traced back to Jessica? She decided she couldn't keep stalling. Life was getting away from her. It was time to act.

Jessica pulled out her instruction sheet and logged on. At first, her screen turned black and then it lit back up. A computer desktop graced her screen, but it was not one she had seen before. She watched and waited for fifteen minutes and there was no action. Impatient, Jessica tried to click one of the desktop icons that looked promising. Nothing happened. It was then she realized that she could see the screen, but she did not have controls over the computer. She could only get information based upon activity, not by searching.

Hungry, she took her laptop into the kitchen and made herself a late lunch, watching the screen for movement in the process. The screen continued to stay steady with no activity present.

By late afternoon, Jessica wasn't sure whether the program was even working properly. She went back through the instructions carefully to see if she missed a step, but she hadn't. Either something wasn't working properly, or there was simply no activity. As she fussed over the situation, a Word document popped up on the screen and words began to appear in the partially completed document. Karen Carter's latest book. She was watching magic happen.

Utterly overwhelmed, Jessica plugged in her laptop and connected it to her big-screen television through Bluetooth. She placed it on the coffee table to keep it within reach and laid down on the couch, the big screen in front of her. She had found her entertainment for the rest of the afternoon and evening.

chapter **eight**

Jessica was mesmerized as she watched the words appear before her. As a writer herself, it was mind-blowing to watch the process of another writer so intimately. It was as raw as she was used to, yet in her head, she had envisioned the words flowing from Karen Carter's mind through her fingers and straight onto the screen, perfectly laid out with no mistakes or awkward sentences. This was not the case. She watched as Karen typed and felt better about her own process, knowing they were similar. Still, she was in awe as she watched the talented writer do what she did best.

Throughout the evening, she continued to watch and Karen had devoted her entire night to writing. Hours passed and Jessica paid no attention as the sun faded outside and the night took over. Suddenly, at nine forty-four p.m., the writing stopped and the word document closed. The screen went blank which she assumed meant Karen's computer had been put to sleep.

Suddenly, realizing her bladder was full, Jessica got up from the couch and used the bathroom. She had lost all track of time. Famished, she made some food and ate it, occasionally checking to see if Karen Carter had started working again, even though while watching earlier, she had noticed the time in the lower-right corner of the screen had been three hours later than California time. There was no further activity and finally, tired from all of the excitement, Jessica turned in for the night.

The next morning, she woke earlier then she usually would, excitement pushing her from the bed. She knew that Karen was three hours ahead of her, so she would need to adjust her schedule to Karen's to make sure she gathered as much information as possible. While she wasn't sure what information she was looking for or how she would use it, she knew that once she saw it, she would simply know.

Jessica took a shower and took care of a few things around the house. After she ate, she sat down at her laptop again and connected. An online banking portal popped up. Intrigued, Jessica tried to figure out what she was looking at as the page scrolled in front of her. It appeared that Karen Carter was paying her bills online. As bills were paid, Jessica saw the checking account balance and felt her breath catch in her throat. There was over a half a million dollars in the checking account alone. She wondered what was available elsewhere in other accounts. Obviously, Karen Carter was doing well for herself.

When Karen was done setting up her bills to pay, Jessica watched as she clicked on the home screen of the account. Confusion overtook her as she saw a name listed there. Lana Brooks. Had she connected to the wrong computer? Her brain told her it was impossible as she had sent the file directly to Karen. It was then that it hit her. Karen Carter must be a pen name. This entire time, she hadn't realized that Karen Carter was actually Lana Brooks.

Her mind spinning, she continued to watch. Karen, or Lana as she was finding out, exited the banking software and brought up email. As she checked her mail, she accessed multiple accounts. Her suspicions were confirmed as some emails were addressed to Lana and some to Karen. They were one and the same.

After a few hours, Jessica watched as Lana

finished what she was doing. When activity stopped for over five minutes, Jessica took a break and started laundry. She continually checked off and on throughout the day until she saw activity again. Lana had started working on her latest novel again. Jessica settled in again for the night to watch, learning everything she could.

Over the next week and a half, Jessica rarely went out. She tried to fit her household activities in between watching what Lana Brooks was doing. During that time, she made quite a few notes on things she learned. Lana wrote every day and had substantial output. She also checked her mail often and occasionally checked the reviews on her books. At one point, Jessica watched as Lana ordered a book through Amazon. When the shipping screen came up, Jessica jotted down Lana's Manhattan address. She now knew where Lana Brooks, aka Karen Carter lived. Not that her address was important. Jessica certainly would never appear on her doorstep and ask her out for coffee.

The more Jessica watched, the more an unfamiliar feeling started to fester. She tried to sort out what was bothering her, but was unable to. She did notice that she felt annoyed and frustrated, but was unable to determine the source.

The following Tuesday, something happened that Jessica had a hard time understanding. She watched as Lana brought up the reviews for some of her latest books and scrolled through them. It was interesting to read what others thought of Lana's Karen Carter books as Jessica had never really checked out the reviews herself. Some of them were wonderful and gave high praise to the author. Others were middle of the road. Then Jessica watched as a one-star review popped up on the screen. She read it at the same time she assumed Lana Brooks was also reading it and was shocked by the content.

I can't believe I wasted two days of my life reading this rubbish. My biggest regret is that I actually finished it. I am stupider now after having read it. The author must have been on a binge of shrooms and drain cleaner, because this book is the worst book I have ever had the displeasure to read. I hope she gets a case of the runs for a week straight and that she can't stay off the toilet. At least then she wouldn't be at her computer writing this tripe.

Shocked at the cruelty of the review, she caught a glimpse of the not-so-glamorous side of being a well-known author. She imagined Lana was reading it and re-reading it, for the review stayed on the screen for many minutes. Finally, when the screen changed, she watched as an Amazon portal popped up. Enthralled, she watched an unfamiliar screen come up and then a page that looked like it contained the name and address of a Kentucky man, Donald Stevens, who was an Amazon customer. Puzzled and having a hard time understanding what was going on, Jessica continued to watch as Lana Googled the name and ran it through several different websites. Jessica jotted down all of the information she saw as it came up, unsure of why it was important, but knowing she may need it. The mystery deepened as she watched Lana pull up a travel website and book a trip to Kentucky.

Jessica was in awe. It made no sense. A reader leaves a bad review on an author's book. Did authors really have the access to the names of the people leaving the reviews? If Donald Stevens was indeed the person that left it, why would she be taking a trip to where he lived? There was no way it could be a coincidence. The trip was in a few days. She would have to keep an eye open for more activity which might explain the event.

Later that evening, Lana worked on her latest novel again. That strange feeling once again took over Jessica's thoughts and she tried harder than ever to break through and figure out the cause. It was then it hit her. Lana Brooks was a great writer, but she was no better or no different than Jessica. She simply was published, because she had managed to make the right contacts. She was shocked to find the strange feeling was actually a growing resentment. She felt ashamed that her reverence for Karen Carter's writing had actually turned to resentment, but the facts were that they were so similar in their work and one of them was successful and one of them wasn't. It just wasn't fair.

Over the next few days, Jessica continued to monitor Lana's activities. On the day the plane ticket had been scheduled for, activity stopped. Lana Brooks was on her way to Kentucky, returning the next day. Anxiety took over as Jessica wondered what was going on, but she knew she would have to simply wait and see if the answers would reveal themselves later.

chapter nine

Jessica stared at her computer screen, shock numbing all of her senses. Donald Stevens was dead—murdered. He had been stabbed through the back of the head with a dagger. The news was all over the Internet. Lana Brooks had to be the murderer. There was no other way to interpret it.

Taking several deep breaths, Jessica tried to calm herself as she worked through what had happened in her mind. A man leaves Karen Carter a shitty review. Lana Brooks blows a gasket over the review, finds out who left it and flies to Kentucky to kill him, then returns home to write more books. Could it really have happened that way?

As she worked through her feelings, she realized she wasn't upset about Donald Stevens dying. Hell, she couldn't count the number of times she fantasized about killing someone that pissed her off. His review was shitty and he was obviously an asshole. What rocked her to the core was that the person she had idolized was just as screwed up as she was. Lana Brooks and she had everything in common. It was almost like they were one and the same.

Later that afternoon, Jessica noticed activity on Lana's computer and watched in awe as her suspicions were confirmed. Lana was pulling up the same internet stories about Donald Stevens that Jessica herself had read earlier in the day. It had to have been Lana.

Even later when Lana resumed writing on her latest novel, Jessica disconnected and sat on the couch, processing all of the new information. She was unable to comprehend what she knew was reality. Confusion clouding her mind, she decided to go to bed and sleep on it.

In the morning, Jessica lay in bed for hours, tossing and turning, not wanting to get up, but unable to sleep any longer. Her sleep throughout the night had been fitful as her mind reeled. Unsure of what the Lana situation meant to her, she continued to try and process it. Did she have a responsibility to report the murder? If she did, would she be single-handedly responsible for crushing the written voice of one of the most prolific authors she knew?

Changed, Jessica took a couple days off from watching Lana's activities and read the very last Karen Carter book that had been published. She had managed to read all of the others in all series. Her emotions were mixed as she enjoyed the story, but knew the person who wrote it wasn't any more deserving than she was. The fact that Lana was also a murderer tainted her thoughts and by the time she finished the book, her mind was racing with different scenarios on how things should play out in Lana's real life.

For the next several weeks, Jessica watched every move that Lana made on the computer. If she was to be honest with herself, it was becoming less about watching and more about stalking. Her love for Karen Carter's books had taken a strange turn and she marveled at how her admiration had turned to resentment and even disdain for Lana Brooks. A fantasy started to play out in Jessica's head on actions she should take to get what she deserved and remedy the situation. If only she had what it took to do something so bold.

In early November, Jessica sunk back deep into her depression. She no longer idolized Karen Carter

—her feelings were more despise—and she worried once again about her money eventually running out. She had information on Lana Brooks that she didn't know what to do with, until one evening when another significant event happened. As Jessica spied on one of Lana's web browsing sessions, she was shocked to find Lana focusing on another one-star review. This one was equally as harsh, titled ***Save Your Money for Something That Doesn't Suck.*** Jessica felt her heart beat rapidly as she anticipated Lana's next move. It played out in front of her as if she had written the script.

Throughout the evening, Jessica watched as Lana researched the name of the customer that had left the review, searched various websites for more information about the person and finally, booked a flight to Dallas, Texas. It was happening again. Lana Brooks was going to Texas and was going to kill a lady named Spring Pastorius.

Typically, not a drinker, Jessica went to the cabinet where she kept a few bottles of liquor for when she had people over, which she realized was never. She broke the wax seal on a bottle of Maker's Mark whiskey and screwed off the lid, pouring herself a double. As she sipped at the strong liquid, her thoughts returned to Lana and the murder she would soon perpetrate.

She stewed over her predicament. Unemployed and funds depleting. Unable to get published. No friends. She had absolutely nothing that mattered to her and Lana Brooks, that murderous bitch, had it all. How was life fair? Why could she never be the one to catch a break?

Not even realizing she had drained the glass, Jessica tried to take a long sip and, coming up empty, she poured herself another one. She was done being forgotten and overlooked. She was something, damnit. She was more than worthless. She would show them. She would show them all.

Feeling no pain, Jessica Nichols booked a flight to Manhattan.

chapter ten

Jessica stared at the Manhattan skyline, taking in the view. Manhattan was a huge culture shock to her as she was used to California. It was certainly colder, but she loved the look and feel of the city. She had arrived mere hours after Lana Brooks had boarded a plane to Texas. She felt alive for the first time in a long time.

Getting into the apartment hadn't been too tricky. A quick call to the superintendent reporting a foul odor coming from the unit had been enough for them to check it out, only to determine there was no odor at all. She had slipped in and hid while the door was open.

Not knowing when Lana would be home, she remained cautious, yet enjoyed her time in the apartment, pretending she was Lana Brooks and Karen

Carter. She could definitely get used to the life Lana lived. On the second day, she remained even more vigilant. Towards evening, she sat in the shadows in the bedroom, waiting and listening. Late that night, she was rewarded with the sound of a key in the lock of the front door. Jessica stood up, smoothed out the bedspread and laid down next to the bed, scooting herself underneath.

Silently concealed in her hiding spot, Jessica noticed the lights come on in the other room and then in the bedroom. From her position, she observed two Nike-adorned feet enter the room, as well as the wheels from a piece of luggage. The corner of the bed sagged as the person she assumed to be Lana sat down and removed her shoes. As she continued to watch, a pile of clothing grew on the floor of the bedroom before the bathroom light kicked on and the apartment's only other occupant disappeared into the adjoining room.

Peering out from her hiding spot, she ensured that she could not be seen from the bathroom before she slipped out from under the bed and took her spot on the corner of the bed, the kitchen knife she had chosen in her hand.

As Jessica waited patiently, her nerves calm, ready to do what she needed to do, Lana clicked off the bathroom light and entered the bedroom, stopping short as soon as she spotted her. The look on Lana's face was one of bewilderment and fear.

"Who the hell are you?" Lana asked through clenched teeth.

"Who do you think I am?" Jessica shot back.

"I'm not into games. Get out now. I'm calling the cops."

"No, you're not. That would be pretty stupid on your part."

Jessica stood up and watched as Lana looked her up and down. Lana's facial expressions made it obvious that she did not know who Jessica was.

Jessica finally spoke again. "Maybe you should call the cops. They may be interested in why you were in Texas."

She watched as Lana tried to hide the shock on her face. "Again, who are you?"

Jessica snickered. "You know me even though you think you don't. I am you."

"What the hell are you talking about?"

"Everything that you are, I am as well," Jessica responded.

Lana was beginning to get frustrated. "Knock it off with the riddles and get out of my house, Bitch!"

"Oh, I'm not leaving, Lana Brooks. Or should I call you Karen Carter?"

Jessica knew she had struck a chord and watched as Lana once again tried to hide her surprise.

"That's right, Ms. Best-Selling Author. Hiding behind your words. Do you think you really deserve all of the praise you've received for your books?"

Lana was getting furious now. "Damn straight, I deserve it. I work my ass off day and night writing to entertain my fans. I deserve way more recognition than I get. I'm the best out there!"

"Opinions vary," Jessica returned, taking a passive-aggressive jab.

"What do you know about writing anyway? Why are you here? This is my house."

"Oh, I know a thing or two about writing. I've written plenty," Jessica informed her.

"And?" Lana challenged.

"And most literary agents are assholes. They don't know a great thing when they see it."

"Or maybe you just suck," Lana said, trying to hit her below the belt.

"Maybe, but I highly doubt it. In fact, many people that have read my work compare me to you. Like I said, I am you. If I suck, then you suck."

Jessica could tell that Lana was about done with the conversation by the look on her face.

"I've had a long day, I'm tired and have very little patience. I want to go to bed. So, tell me, Ms. Great-Little-Writer, what do you want from me?" Lana asked.

"I want people to save their money for something that doesn't suck." Jessica knew she had hit home.

"Why did you just say that?" Lana asked. "Once again, what is it you really want?"

"You don't deserve what you have, Lana . . . Karen . . . whatever the hell your name is."

"I have worked hard for everything I have!" Lana screamed, finally out of patience. "When I was a nobody—like you are—I promised myself that I would do whatever it took to make it to the big time. Now I'm here and I'm not going to let some blonde bitch screw with me."

Jessica watched as Lana took a step towards her.

"So, whatever it takes, huh?" Jessica stood her ground. "Even killing someone?"

Lana stopped in her tracks. Jessica could see the rage in her body project through her eyes.

Jessica continued. "That's what I thought. You'd kill to be successful. While that doesn't surprise me, I have something that might surprise you."

Lana sneered. “Fine. I’ll bite. What’s that?”

“I’m no different than you. I AM you, and I also will do anything it takes.”

As Jessica brought the steely-cold boning knife up from her side, she saw the look of panic in Lana’s eyes.

“What are you saying?” Lana asked, taking a step backwards. “You’d kill to be successful?”

“You catch on quickly, don’t you?”

“How is killing me going to help your writing career?”

“Maybe less competition would help?” Jessica offered. “Do you like blades? Something tells me you do.”

Unexpectantly, Jessica watched as Lana lunged towards her, unable to move out of the way. Pain radiated throughout her wrist and she screamed as Lana twisted. The knife clattered to the floor, the metal thudding sharply against the hardwood slats. The force of Lana lunging at her caused them both to go down, bounce off the corner of the bed and hit the floor. Lana landed on top of her and she gasped as she tried to breathe air back into her lungs.

Jessica was surprised at how quickly Lana had attacked her and before she realized it, Lana’s hands were around her throat. She struggled desperately to get free, but Lana's grip was tight and determined.

Unable to breathe and knowing the end was near if she could not get the upper hand, Jessica dropped her arms to her side and went still, letting her eyes roll inside her head. She felt the grip relax ever-so-slightly and as it did, she extended her fingers to the last place she had seen the knife. She was rewarded as the cold steel kissed her fingertips. Knowing she would pass out soon, Jessica grabbed the knife and struck quickly, drawing the blade violently across Lana's arm. She was rewarded immediately as she was released from the grip and she took advantage of the moment by popping back to her feet, a choreography taking place between them of knife-wielding maniac trying to land the blade in Lana's flesh and intended victim dancing diligently away from the dangerous object.

Determined to end things before Lana got the upper hand, Jessica once again rushed her, this time going for the heart. Everything happened in slow motion and once again, she found her wrist being twisted around and the instantaneous pain caused her to release the blade again. What surprised Jessica even more was the speed and dexterity that Lana exhibited when she rushed in and picked up the knife off the floor, well before Jessica could even react. The hunted had become the hunter.

"What now, Bitch?" Lana sneered. "Looks like you will continue to be the loser you are."

Jessica rushed at Lana and tried to take the knife away, watching in horror as Lana lifted the knife up in front of her. Her momentum carried her forward, even as she tried to change direction, but she could not stop what was in motion and as a sickening feeling took over, she realized that she was going to die. She didn't even comprehend that the knife had buried itself in her flesh to the hilt, as she fell to the floor.

Knowing it was over, Jessica lay still, waiting for whatever would be coming for her to take her away to a future unknown. Her blurred vision caught Lana sliding onto the floor. It was the open crying and wailing from Lana that caught her attention. She was still there. Still alive. Death had not yet come to carry her away.

Not feeling the pain that she knew she should be feeling, Jessica listened to Lana cry uncontrollably as her peripheral vision caught her rocking back and forth in a sitting position.

Minutes later, Jessica realized that she still hadn't died and watched as Lana Brooks pulled herself up from the floor and walked over to the phone, her back to Jessica. As Lana dialed, Jessica gathered all of her strength and silently pulled herself up from the floor, extracted the knife from her gut and slid up behind Lana, before drawing the blade effortlessly across her throat. As Lana slid to the floor in front of her, her eyes wide, Jessica grabbed the phone from her hand and put it to her ear.

"Hello? Is anyone there? This is nine-one-one. What's your emergency? Hello?"

chapter eleven

Standing on her new balcony looking at the Manhattan skyline, the glass of champagne went down way too easy. Jessica poured another glass. She had reason to celebrate. Her latest Karen Carter book was a bestseller and was getting rave reviews. She couldn't be happier.

Getting to this place in her life hadn't been easy. Writing was a tough gig, but she knew she had the grit to do whatever it would take to make it happen. She had done just that.

Reflecting back to that night three months ago—the night she almost lost her life—she had no regrets. Being attacked with the knife was scary, but she had won. She came out on top.

The hospital did a great job of stitching her up

and although it took some time to heal—both physically and emotionally—she used the incident to fuel her writing, churning out over five thousand words per day.

Coming inside from the balcony, she went into the bathroom, peeled off her shirt and looked at the scar. It would definitely be a conversation starter. Her gaze wandered up to her face and she analyzed her expression. She felt happy and she felt like she *looked* happy. A little murder wouldn't detract from her cheerfulness.

She remembered the body. After the call was made to the nine-one-one dispatcher, she had hidden it, cleaned up the scene and took the elevator down to the lobby to wait for the ambulance. She took the knife with her to show them what had hurt her, as well as demonstrate how she had accidentally injured herself by falling with the knife in her hand. They bought the story and after she was fixed up, she was released and was able to return home.

Back in the Manhattan apartment, it took her two days, but she was able to drain the blood from Lana's body, dismember it and place it in a dozen different trash bags. She hoped that by strategically dumping the bags down the three different trash-chutes located around the building, the body parts would hit the landfill undetected. After three months, she was pretty sure she had gotten away with it. There were no reports of found body parts on the news.

Grateful for everything she had, she went to her new office and examined the custom built-in bookcase that lined one wall. All of the Karen Carter books were there and she took time to admire them, running her fingers down many of the spines. She selected the latest one and opened the cover. Best-selling author. Award winning. She was rich. She was famous. She was Karen Carter.

Her thoughts once again flashed back to that night. The knife to the gut, buried to the handle. The blood. The pain. It was unfathomable to her that she had remained still after taking the six-inch blade. Lana had bought her possum act. She shuddered with pleasure as she reflected on how she had pulled the knife from her body and sliced Lana's throat with it. It was all over quickly.

Jessica Nichols looked enough like Lana Brooks that the hospital did not question the identification she presented, which she had taken out of Lana's purse after she died. Lana had no family and her friends were not close by. No one knew what Karen Carter looked like, so Jessica simply took over Lana's life and continued to write using her voice. Jessica Nichols *was* Lana Brooks and she *was* Karen Carter.

She smiled to herself, knowing she had committed the perfect crime. The world was now hers and no one would ever tell her she wasn't good enough.

In love with her new life and career, Jessica checked the daily sales for her latest release and felt giddy. It was doing better than anyone had expected. Even she had no idea what to expect, but this was beyond her wildest dreams.

Inspired, Jessica looked at the review section on Amazon to see if any new ones had populated. She loved to read the praise the readers heaped upon her and the book. So far, the book had three hundred and twenty-seven reviews. Four of them were left since she checked the prior night. She read the first one. Four stars and overall a strong review. The second one raved about the book and the reader gave five stars. As Jessica got to the third one, she felt her face burn and it became difficult to breathe. A one-star review. She read the comments and her anger surged.

"Stupid cow!" she muttered, under her breath. "I'll teach you to mess with me."

Jessica reached in the desk drawer and pulled out a notebook. She found the notes Lana had left for her own records. She knew they would come in handy some day and that time was now. Smiling, Jessica logged into the employee account assigned to Lana's ex-boyfriend. She couldn't wait to give the one-star reviewer a response she wasn't expecting.

the karen carter series continues

author's note

Becoming Karen Carter is the second book in the **Karen Carter Series**, following the book **One-Star Review**. To see where it all started, pick up **One-Star Review** from any online bookseller.

about the author

R.E. Sargent is the author of three novels, four novelettes, and many short stories in the genres of suspense, supernatural, and horror. He is an active member of the Horror Writers Association, the Alliance of Independent Authors, and the Community of Literary Magazines and Presses. His short story, "Lucy," was featured in the 2021 Splatterpunk Award–nominated anthology *If I Die Before I Wake Volume 3 – Tales of Deadly Women and Retribution.*

R.E. lives in the Pacific Northwest with his wife and their Chocolate Lab. And the rain. Lots and lots of rain. He is thankful that writing is an indoor activity.

Correspondence to the author should be directed to any of the following:

facebook.com/r.e.sargentofficial

www.resargent.com

Made in United States
Troutdale, OR
08/13/2026

52329332R00059